ISBN 978-0-06-241106-8

The artist used India ink on vellum to create the illustrations for this book.
Typography by Rick Farley
18 19 20 PC 10 9 8 7 6 5 4
❖
First Edition

This book is for Michael.

I AM A STORY

By Dan Yaccarino

HARPER
An Imprint of HarperCollinsPublishers

I am a story.

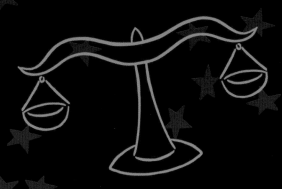

I was told around a campfire,

then painted on cave walls.

I was carved onto clay tablets

and told in pictures.

I was written on papyrus

and printed with ink and woodblocks,

then woven into tapestries

and copied into big books to illuminate minds.

I was printed and bound,

then acted out onstage.

I was read in vast private libraries,

then in public libraries open to everyone,

and in places you'd never imagine.

I made people frightened,

excited,

sad,

and happy.

I was censored,

banned,

I've inspired millions.

I can go with you everywhere

and will live forever.

I am a story.

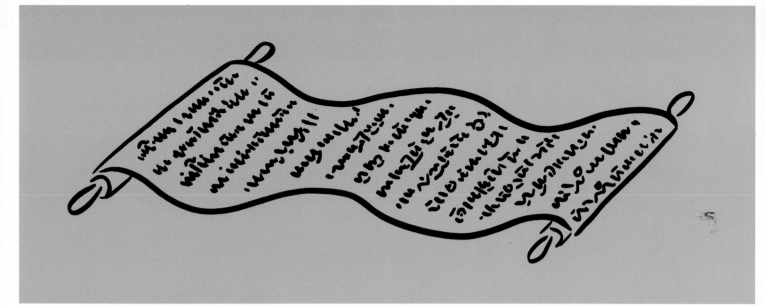

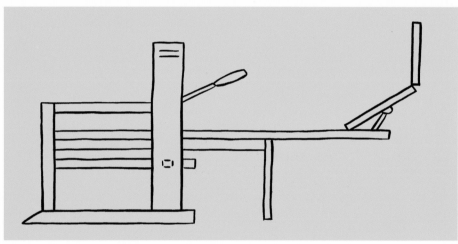